Dedication:

FOR WEDNESDAY "MASTERLIMIKER",
MATEO, AND ENRIQUE.

MAY YOU ALWAYS STRIVE FOR HAPPINESS ABOVE ALL THINGS.

FOR THE PEOPLE INSPIRED BY "RICH DAD, POOR DAD,"
MAY YOUR CHILDREN LEARN A LESSON FROM THIS BOOK.

WISDOM BOOKS

www.WisdomBooksUSA.com

ADVENTURES OF
P, B, AND J:

BE IN CONTROL
OF YOUR EMOTIONS

BY: CARL CUESTA

ILLUSTRATED BY: MARIA RODRIGUEZ

Benjamin was one of the kindest giraffes in the deep African forest.

It was his affectionate nature that helped him make new friends and end quarrels between animal communities.

It was due to his gentleness that Jackson and Penny were so close him as friends and the three of them lived happily under a beautiful tree.

However there was one thing that made Benjamin very unhappy.

It was a losing something precious to him, like the scarf that his mom had knit for him on last Christmas.

Alex the monkey was known for his mischievous nature and everyone tended to stay away from him due to that very reason.

One day Alex saw Benjamin's scarf that he was folding with love.

Being a naughty monkey that he was, he stole that scarf!

When Benjamin looked for it and couldn't find it,
he became sad.

He began to question his best friends, Penny and Jackson
about it.

But neither of them knew where the scarf was.

From far away, Alex saw this situation and laughed happily.

With each passing day Benjamin became angrier and angrier, until his friends and all the other animals began to avoid him.

They used to whisper that the once happy and kind Benjamin was lost and in his place a grumpy giraffe was always stomping the ground.

Seeing him this way, Penny and Jackson went to the animal court to find the culprit and punish him for his actions.

The wise owls put a few foxes on this mission and they found that Alex had stolen the scarf.

"Alex the monkey, we have found this scarf from your house and it belongs to Benjamin, the giraffe!

Why did you commit this crime?" Mr. Owl asked Alex.

"Benjamin was fond of this scarf and I saw it and became jealous.

So I stole it to hurt him", Alex told the truth.

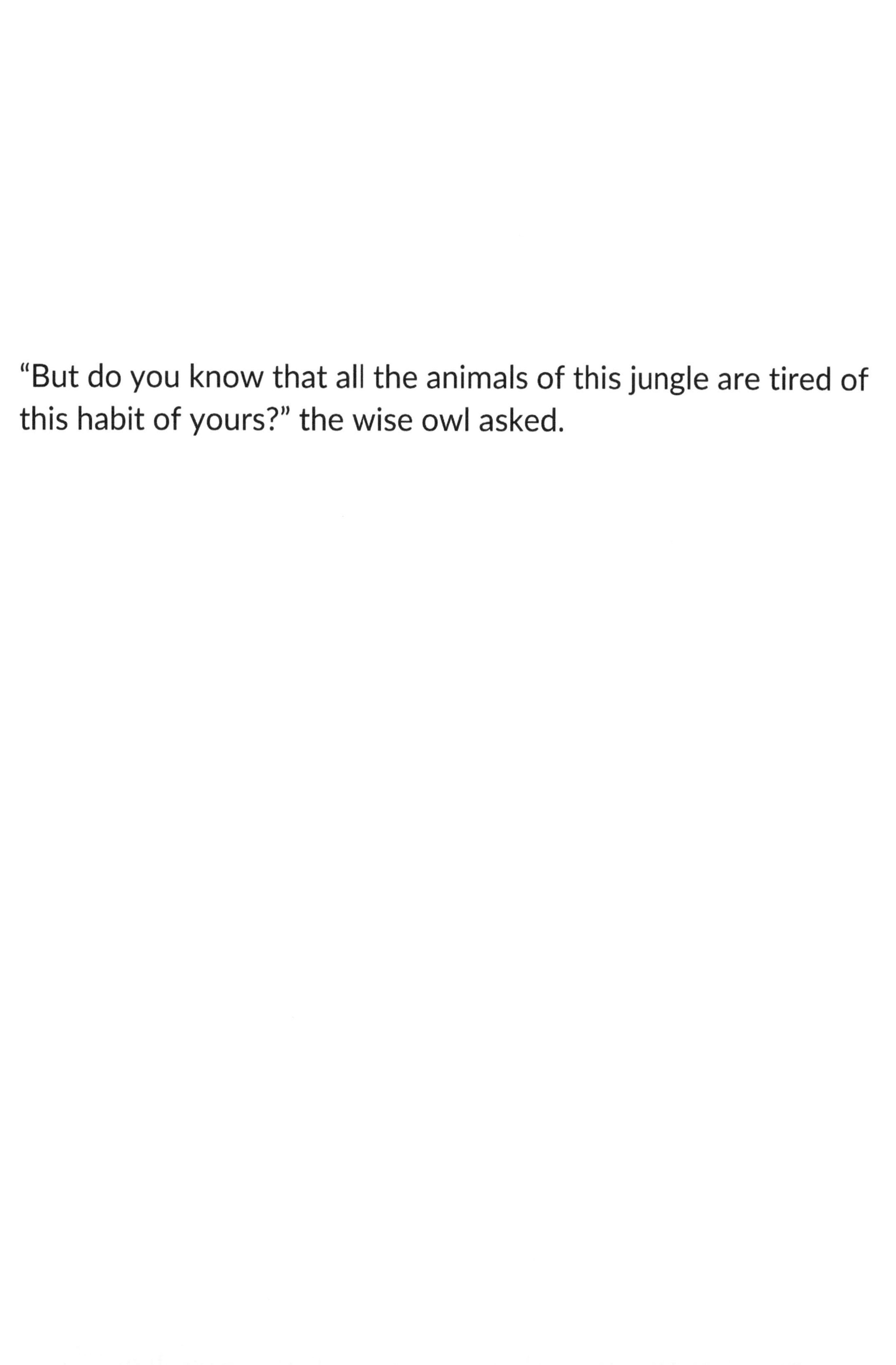

"But do you know that all the animals of this jungle are tired of this habit of yours?" the wise owl asked.

Learning this, Alex became very ashamed of his actions and begged for forgiveness.

He was forgiven on a condition that he would be a good monkey from now onwards.

"As for you Benjamin, all the animals loved you.

But ever since that scarf was stolen, you became so angry, that you hurt everybody with your words, even your best friends.

We must **always control our emotions** and make sure that we don't hurt anybody with our actions", Mr. Owl concluded.

"I am so sorry everybody.

I know that I made all of you very sad because of my actions and my hurtful words when I was angry.

But I promise that from now onwards I will always be the Benjamin you know", Benjamin said with determination.

Everyone cheered listening to his words and understanding
that no matter how angry we are,

we should not hurt anyone else ,

as the pain inflicted by those words stays with us forever.

THE END